P9-CKL-092

CALGARY PUBLIC LIBRARY

AUG    2016

Dear Parents and Educators,

Welcome to Penguin Young Readers! As parents and educators, you know that each child develops at his or her own pace—in terms of speech, critical thinking, and, of course, reading. Penguin Young Readers recognizes this fact. As a result, each Penguin Young Readers book is assigned a traditional easy-to-read level (1–4) as well as a Guided Reading Level (A–P). Both of these systems will help you choose the right book for your child. Please refer to the back of each book for specific leveling information. Penguin Young Readers features esteemed authors and illustrators, stories about favorite characters, fascinating nonfiction, and more!

## Noah's Ark

**LEVEL 2**

GUIDED READING LEVEL **I**

This book is perfect for a **Progressing Reader** who:
• can figure out unknown words by using picture and context clues;
• can recognize beginning, middle, and ending sounds;
• can make and confirm predictions about what will happen in the text; and
• can distinguish between fiction and nonfiction.

Here are some **activities** you can do during and after reading this book:
• —ed Endings: List all the words in the story that have an —ed ending. On a separate piece of paper, write the root word next to the word with the —ed ending. The chart below will get you started:

| Word with an -ed Ending | Root Word |
| --- | --- |
| lived | live |
| loved | love |
| talked | talk |

• Comprehension: After reading the story, use your memory to answer the following questions:
  • How old is Noah at the beginning of the story?
  • Who tells Noah to build an ark?
  • What kind of animal brings Noah an olive branch?

Remember, sharing the love of reading with a child is the best gift you can give!

—Bonnie Bader, EdM
  Penguin Young Readers program

*Penguin Young Readers are leveled by independent reviewers applying the standards developed by Irene Fountas and Gay Su Pinnell in *Matching Books to Readers: Using Leveled Books in Guided Reading*, Heinemann, 1999.

For Micah and Zoe—AR

To Carlos, Marc, and Claudia. Thanks for
being by my side every day—MC

PENGUIN YOUNG READERS

An Imprint of Penguin Random House LLC

Penguin supports copyright. Copyright fuels creativity, encourages diverse voices,
promotes free speech, and creates a vibrant culture. Thank you for buying an authorized
edition of this book and for complying with copyright laws by not reproducing, scanning,
or distributing any part of it in any form without permission. You are supporting writers and
allowing Penguin to continue to publish books for every reader.

Copyright © 2016 by Penguin Random House LLC. All rights reserved.
Published by Penguin Young Readers, an imprint of Penguin Random House LLC, 345 Hudson Street,
New York, New York 10014. Manufactured in China.

*Library of Congress Cataloging-in-Publication Data is available.*

ISBN 978-0-448-48967-4 (pbk)          10 9 8 7 6 5 4 3 2 1
ISBN 978-0-448-48968-1 (hc)           10 9 8 7 6 5 4 3 2 1

PENGUIN YOUNG READERS

LEVEL 2
PROGRESSING
READER

# NOAH'S ARK

by Avery Reed
illustrated by Marta Costa

Penguin Young Readers
An Imprint of Penguin Random House

A long time ago,

there lived a man named Noah.

Noah was 500 years old.

He and his wife had three sons.

Each son had a wife.

Many people lived near Noah.

They did lots of bad things.

They hurt one another.

They did not listen to God.

This made God very sad.

God loved his people.

Noah was different

from the others.

Noah loved God.

God was his friend.

Noah spent time with God

and talked to him every day.

One day, God told Noah

he was going to make it rain.

It was going to rain so much

that water would cover

the whole earth.

God told Noah to build an ark.

An ark is a big boat.

God said he would save Noah

and his family from the storm.

He would also save

two of every kind of animal.

Noah did not know how

to make an ark.

But God did.

He told Noah how to build it.

All of Noah's friends

laughed at him.

They thought it would never rain.

But Noah trusted God.

It took Noah many years

to build the ark.

Finally, it was ready.

Noah was now over 600 years old.

He and his family

climbed into the ark.

Two animals of every kind

also climbed in!

Some walked.

Others hopped.

And others flew.

Some barked.

Others roared.

And others cooed.

It was very crowded!

Then God closed the door.

After seven days,

it began to rain.

And rain.

And rain.

And rain.

It rained for 40 days
and 40 nights.
Water covered the whole earth,
even the tips
of the tallest mountains.

At last, the rain stopped.

Noah opened a window.

He let out a dove.

The dove flew very far.

But she could not find

a place to land.

The earth was still under

the water.

So the dove flew back to Noah.

Noah waited seven more days.

Then he let the dove

fly out again.

This time, the dove came back
to Noah with an olive branch.
She had found a tree.
The water was going down!

The ark had landed

on the top of a mountain.

God told Noah it was safe to get

out of the ark.

Noah, his family, and all the
animals walked out onto
dry land.

The first thing Noah did

was thank God.

God had kept them safe

during the storm.

30

Then God made a promise

to Noah.

God said he would never

make a flood cover

the whole earth again.

Then Noah looked up.

There was a huge rainbow

in the sky!

God said it was a sign

that he would never, ever

break his promise.